The New Neighbours

Story by Julie Ellis

Illustrations by Naomi C. Lewis

Contents

Chapter 1
The Neighbours Move In

Emma could see the new neighbours moving in next door.

"Come and look, Matthew," she called. "There's a bike and some balls."

"They must have children," said Matthew, "because that looks like a trampoline."

"It will be fun to have some new children to play with," said Emma.

The next day, Emma and Matthew
heard a noise coming from over the fence.

A boy was jumping on the trampoline,
and counting loudly.

"Hello," called Emma.

The boy didn't look at Emma.
He kept jumping and counting.

"Why didn't he hear us?" asked Matthew.

Chapter 2

Dan

A woman came out of the house.
"Hello," said the woman.
"My name is Clare, and this is my son, Dan."

"Hello, Dan," called Matthew.
"Would you like to play with us?"

Dan still didn't look at Emma and Matthew.
"I like number ten," he said.
Then he jumped off the trampoline
and walked away.

"Dan didn't mean to be rude," said Clare.
"He has autism, so he doesn't think
in the same way as most children.
Dan loves maths,
but he doesn't know how to talk to people."

"Can he play games?" asked Matthew.

"Dan doesn't know how to play games
with other children," said Clare.
"And he doesn't have any brothers or sisters
to teach him."

That gave Emma an idea.

"We could teach Dan how to play games,"
Emma said to Matthew.
"You could kick balls with Dan,
and I could play other games with him."

"He may not like us," said Matthew.
"Then he won't want to play at all."

"Well, I'm going to try," said Emma.

Chapter 3

The Number Game

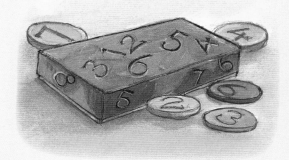

Emma ran inside
and found her number game.
Then she went over to see Clare and Dan.

"This is a great idea," said Clare.
"Thank you, Emma."

But Dan wouldn't play with Emma.
He walked away.

Emma sat on the floor by herself.
She counted loudly
as she moved the counters.
"One, two, three, four," she said.

Dan came back and sat down near Emma.
"One, two, three, four," he said,
and he looked at the game.

Matthew was playing with his racing cars when Emma got home.

"Did Dan play a game with you?" asked Matthew.

"Yes," said Emma. "He likes numbers."

"Dan will like my cars," said Matthew. "They have all got numbers on them."